the Adventures of

Ralph Rabbit

Louise T. Constantinople

Illustrations by Terry Pond

outskirtspress
DENVER, COLORADO

The Adventures of Ralph Ribbit
All Rights Reserved.
Copyright © 2012 Louise T. Constantinople
V2.0 R1.0

Cover Illustration © 2012 Terry Pond . All rights reserved - used with permission.
Interior Illustrations © 2012 Outskirts Press, Inc. All Rights Reserved. Used with permission.

Outskirts Press, Inc.
http://www.outskirtspress.com

ISBN: 978-1-4327-8853-7

Outskirts Press and the "OP" logo are trademarks belonging to Outskirts Press, Inc.

PRINTED IN THE UNITED STATES OF AMERICA

Table of Contents

Chapter One

The Missing Directions

RALPH RIBBIT WAS in a panic. He leapt around the den of his lily pad, his round black eyes darting here and there as he tossed papers, books and kids' toys out of his way. His forehead was furrowed into creases, and the slight upward curve of his mouth, which gave Ralph his kindly expression, was turned upside down.

"Where is it? Where is it? I know it was around here somewhere," Ralph croaked. He looked under his armchair; nothing but a few dried leaves. Then he checked under his morning newspaper, which lay spread out on the table next to the chair. Not there either. He was already off to a late start; now he was wasting more time searching for the map of the stream. But somehow it had gone missing. Not a good start to his day or his trip.

Ralph lived with his wife and two children on a large lily pad near the bank of a quiet stream. Rocks of all sizes dotted the water for as far as the eye could see. Tall grasses and reeds grew from the damp earth near the water's edge. Leafy trees lined the stream bank and provided a shade cover from the hot afternoon sun. At dawn and dusk, dragonflies, gnats, lightning bugs and flies swarmed overhead, offering Ralph and the other frog families living there an endless variety of ready-to-eat meals. And although he had to leave the peace of his pad to go to work every day, Ralph preferred to stay close to home with his family whenever he could.

But that was not the case today. Soon he would be on his way to *Leaps and Bounds,* a sports equipment and clothing store for frogs. Jack Stone, the school's track coach, had ordered uniform shirts for his team to wear at the championship meet that Saturday. Jack had planned to pick them up himself, but he'd slipped on a wet rock and sprained his foot. A trip to the doctor's office had changed his plans.

"Stay off that foot for at least a week," the doctor warned, "or your sprain will get worse. No swimming or jumping, Mr. Stone. None."

When Ralph heard that Coach Stone was not able to make the trip to *Leaps and Bounds* to get the shirts, he knew Reggie and the rest of the team would be disappointed, so he had offered to go in Jack's place. But the store was far up the stream in an area that was unfamiliar to Ralph and riddled with forks that split it in two directions. Coach Stone, who had been to the sports store several times before and knew the way there, drew a detailed map for him to follow. Ralph had looked it over quickly when he got home, but now it was nowhere to be found.

What could have happened to it? he wondered.

Ralph was still searching for the missing paper when his wife Ramona appeared in the den doorway. She had just returned home from her job as the manager of *The Webbed Foot*, a beauty salon that offered webbicures and skin polishing to the frog and toad population in the neighborhood. Ramona was capable and confident, which made her a good manager. But more importantly, she was devoted to her family, which made her a good wife to Ralph and a great mother to Reggie and his younger sister Roxanne.

"Good heavens, Ralph! What's going on here?" she said. "You've practically trashed the place. What are you looking for?" Her golden eyes took in the mess he had made of the room.

"The sheet of directions to *Leaps and Bounds* ! I know I had it last night, but now it's gone," Ralph said, shaking his head slowly. "I'm beginning to wonder if it was such a good idea for me to volunteer to pick up the team shirts when I don't know how to get to the store."

"You volunteered to go because you're always the first frog to help someone who needs it. And you also know how important it is to Reggie and all the other 6th grade frogs to have shirts that make them feel more like a team," Ramona said, kissing his cheek. "But most of all because you're a good dad."

"Well, dear, let's see how good I am at finding my way upstream and back again without those directions."

Ramona patted Ralph on the shoulder. "Just take your time.

— 4 —

You'll get there. I know you will." Ralph smiled at his wife. She always had faith in him even when he doubted himself.

"I hope you're right, Ramona." He looked around the room one final time and sighed.

"Well, I don't have any more time to spend looking for them. I took two days off from work, and now I'll need every minute of them."

Ralph worked at the Acme Bug Company, a large laboratory that collected many types of bugs and studied their make-up and behavior. As head of Insect Analysis, Ralph supervised a team of four other scientists. They were very busy right now, what with the larvae hatching and all. He and his team were working on an important dragonfly project, and Ralph worried that it wasn't a good time for him to ask his boss to be away from the lab. But Reggie was proud that Ralph had offered to help the team in such an important way, so he gathered the courage to ask Mr. Rupert for the time off. A family frog himself, Ralph's boss understood why he wanted to go.

"The chance to do something like this doesn't come along very often. Your son will remember that you cared enough to run this errand for his team much longer than he'll remember any of the toys you bought him," Mr. Rupert said. "Besides, Ralph, you've trained your team well. They can carry on without you for two days."

Ralph was thinking about how grateful he was to have a boss like Wilson Rupert when Ramona reached behind his favorite chair and handed Ralph's backpack to him.

"Okay. Everything you'll need for the trip is in here: moisturizing cream for your skin, a jacket and blanket if it gets chilly, your sunglasses, and a couple of snack bags of grasshopper and gnat trail mix."

As she helped Ralph sling the heavy pack over his shoulders, she added, "Oh, before I forget. I put the 85 packages of dried flies that Coach gave you to pay for the shirts in an envelope in the inside pocket of your jacket. Make sure you check every so often to see that it hasn't fallen out." Ramona kissed her husband's cheek again. "You'd better get going, dear, and be careful."

Ralph walked to the door and paused. "Gee Ramona, I wish Reggie and Roxanne weren't in school right now. I didn't have the chance to say goodbye to them. And I won't be here to tell Roxie a bedtime story, either."

Roxie was six years old and looked just like her mother- petite, with light green skin and big round eyes. Ralph's heart did flip flops every time she hopped out the front door to meet him when he came home from work. He had started telling her nightly bedtime stories when she was just out of the tadpole stage, and Ralph had seldom missed a night since then. He smiled as he thought about her, and he wondered who looked forward to that time more, Roxanne or himself.

"I'll tell Roxie a story… or maybe Reggie will do it. Don't worry. We'll manage," Ramona said, knowing how it would bother Ralph not to be there for his daughter.

"Yes, yes okay," he said, as he gave his wife a quick hug. "See you in a couple of days. I'll get there one way or another. I don't want to let Reggie and the team down. Give the kids my love." And with that, Ralph hopped out the door and headed to the water's edge. He was on his way.

Chapter Two
Ralph's Journey Begins

THE LATE MORNING sun beat down on Ralph's head as he made his way along the edge of the stream. His red backpack bounced up and down on his shoulders, its weight slowing him down as he hopped through the tall grasses and rocks that lined its banks. He paused when he reached the fence that surrounded the schoolyard, hoping to catch a glimpse of his children out on the playground. But it was empty. *Probably too close to lunchtime*, Ralph thought, disappointed. Sighing, he continued on his way.

He'd been traveling for several minutes when he noticed one of his neighbors sweeping the scum off his lily pad with a broom. It was Dewey Travis, the father of one of the boys on Reggie's track team. Although he really didn't have time to stop and talk, Dewey had already spotted Ralph, dropped the broom, and bounded toward him.

"Hey, Ralph. Long time no see," he said in his booming voice. "What brings you here? Don't usually see you this far up the stream." Ralph knew Dewey could talk the ears off a rabbit, so he replied politely, but in as few words as possible.

"Hello Dewey. I'm on my way to pick up the team shirts for Saturday's meet."

"Oh yeah, I remember somebody tellin' me that Coach Stone asked for a volunteer to go pick 'em up 'cause he couldn't do it. If I'da known about it, I woulda offered to go pick 'em up myself. Coach and me go way back, y'know. And he really likes my kid Eddy-- thinks he's the best runner on the team. Coach picked him specially as anchor for the relay event, y'know."

When Ralph didn't comment, Dewey continued to question him.

"So where you goin' to get the shirts?"

"*Leaps and Bounds*," Ralph said.

"Geez, that place is far away. I know a place that's a lot closer—place called *Archie's Track Shack* . My brother used them coupla years ago when his kid's team needed track shoes. Guy there gave him a good price, too. What's it gonna cost ya at that place?"

Ralph didn't want to get into the details of the purchase, but he answered Dewey's question, hoping it would end the conversation.

"85 packages of dried flies."

"Oh, geez, that's expensive. If Coach hadda called me, I

coulda got them for way less at *Archie's*. The owner'd go outta his way to give me the cheapest price 'cause he knows my brother. Too bad Coach didn't check with me first."

"Yes, well, maybe next time," Ralph said. " I've really got to get going, Dewey. I'm not familiar with this part of the stream, and I heard that it twists and splits up ahead."

"Yeah, it sure does. I know this area like the spots on my skin. I could get there with no problem."

"Really?" Ralph said. "Since you know the stream so well, would you come along with me? I'd really appreciate it."

"Oh geez, Ralph, you know I would if I could, but I got a million things goin' on around here. You know, yard work, an' stuff with my kid. The wife has me hoppin' around every minute, too. But I hope you have good luck findin' the place. Nice seein' ya, though," Dewey said, and hopped back to pick up his broom.

It would have been helpful to have Dewey show him the way upstream, but Ralph was more relieved than disappointed that Dewey was not going with him. His non-stop bragging irritated Ralph, but he was willing to put up with it if it meant making his trip easier. Since Ralph had planned to make the journey on his own anyway, he was no worse off than before he'd spoken to Dewey.

He continued past the long line of lily pads that sat at the water's edge. Groups of froglets played hopscotch and leapfrog in the afternoon sun. Every once in a while, they would jump, squeaking and splashing, into the cool stream water. Their joyous play made Ralph wonder if his own children were doing the same thing at home. He missed them already.

Tired and hungry from his travel, Ralph decided to rest in a thicket of lush grass and cattails swaying gently in the breeze. Several moss-covered rocks jutted out into the water, making a perfect spot for him to sit and have a snack. He sat at the edge of the largest rock, waiting to lunge at a few hovering mosquitoes or gnats. He would catch them, one at a time, on his sticky, outstretched tongue and swallow them whole. Ralph could have eaten one of the snack bags Ramona had packed for him, but he wanted to save them just in case he needed them later.

Tummy full, Ralph decided to spend a few minutes resting on the rock. The trickle of water flowing over it was calming. And without realizing it, Ralph fell sound asleep, as several hours of daylight slipped away.

Chapter Three
Crow Cove

A CHILLY BREEZE awakened Ralph, and he sat up with a start. The sun was no longer in the sky, and dusk had fallen. The few minutes he had meant to spend relaxing on the mossy rock had turned into hours, and he was angry for wasting the daylight sleeping.

"How could I have let this happen?" he scolded himself.

Over the burbling of the water, he heard crickets chirping and cicadas humming. The trees looked like black leafy giants against the purple sky. Where land ended and water began was now a blurry line.

"Even with my good eyesight, finding my way in the dark will be harder now," he said.

Ralph dug into his backpack to check that nothing had fallen out, especially the envelope with the payment for the team shirts. Satisfied that he had everything, Ralph hoisted the pack over his shoulders and jumped into the water, moving with ease. His muscular body, with its strong hind legs and webbed feet, pumped water like a machine.

Ralph's nap had given him new energy, and he swam until he reached a fork in the stream. A large area of land, covered with dry leaves and twigs, rose up out of the water, which flowed around the mass on either side.

"Which way should I go?" he wondered. Ralph hopped onto the muddy grass at the edge of the mound and sat down under a nearby tree to think. Suddenly, something hard hit him on the head.

"Ouch!" he cried, looking up. He saw nothing but tangled branches, and thought that he might have imagined it. And then… *thonk.* And again. *Thonk.* Sure that he was not imagining things, Ralph tilted his head back a second time. Still he saw nothing.

It was when he heard muffled snickering above him that he knew someone was using his head for target practice. He sat very still, waiting to get hit again. He did. An acorn bounced off his head onto his lap.

Just who is it that thinks this is so funny? Ralph thought angrily.

"Who's up there?" he called into the trees. No reply. "What's going on here?" Still no answer.

He was about to shout again when he heard cackling behind him. Startled because the sound had moved, Ralph turned to see two black crows rolling around on their backs in the grass, laughing.

"Boy, we got you good, didn't we? Those acorns make great ammo. And we never miss our target," the larger of the two chortled.

The crows moved to stand in front of Ralph. It was the smaller of the two that spoke. "What are you doin' here? Don't you know this is Crow Cove? That means *crows only*. Read the sign," he said, flicking his beak toward the water's edge.

Ralph turned and saw a weathered wooden board that was tied to a tree branch and stuck into the mud. Printed in bird's foot letters, the sign read: **CROW COVE. NO TRESPASSERS. THAT MEANS YOU!**

"Oh, I'm very sorry," Ralph said, embarrassed that he had not bothered to read it. "I didn't realize this was private property. You see, I'm on my way to a store far upstream on an errand for my son's track coach, and I misplaced the directions he'd given me. When I saw the fork in the stream, I hopped onto your island to decide which way I should go."

"Yeah, well, we usually don't like uninvited company," the larger crow said as he took a step closer to Ralph.

"The name's Marcus. And he's Maurice," he said, flapping a wing at his friend. "We bop trespassers on the noggin with a few nuts to get them movin' again. Usually works, too. Most of 'em don't stick around after that. So who are you, anyway?"

" My name is Ralph Ribbit, and I assure you I mean no harm. I'll just be on my way now."

Ralph made a move to jump back into the water when the large black bird stepped in front of him. Marcus was used to acting on instinct, the little voice inside of him that told him who to fear or who meant no harm. It was this instinct, or maybe something in the frog's quiet manner, that told Marcus that Ralph was not a threat.

"Now, now, Ralph, hold on a minute," he said, his tone becoming more friendly. "I said we *usually* don't like strangers here, but once in a while, we make an exception. Isn't that right, Maurice?"

Marcus glanced at the smaller crow. Maurice had been his assistant for a long time and had never known him to make an exception to the "no trespassing" rule. He seldom allowed even a strange *crow* to stay on the island, much less a lost frog. But Marcus was the boss, so Maurice just nodded his agreement.

From the time he had arrived at Crow Cove, Marcus had made it clear to the rest of the crows that he was their leader. The rules he made would be followed without question or argument. His size and manner frightened the Cove's inhabitants, and they quietly obeyed the huge bird.

Maurice was the smallest crow on the cove. Not only was he fearful of the other crows, but was especially afraid of Marcus. Surprised when Marcus chose to befriend him, Maurice was relieved when he promised to protect him from harm in exchange for his unquestioning loyalty. And now, although he wanted to ask Marcus about his sudden change of heart, Maurice knew better, and certainly not in front of the stranger. As Crow Cove's leader, if Marcus made the rules then he could break them, too.

"Well, I really do need to be on my way. I'm already behind schedule, and I don't want to lose any more time—or take up any more of yours," Ralph said.

"Let me tell you, Ralph, this stream is real hard to follow, especially in the dark. There're twists and forks in it all the way along. Chances are, if you leave now, you're sure to get lost," Marcus said.

" You know, you seem okay, even for a frog. Why don't you hang around here tonight and leave in the daylight? You can camp out anywhere you want," Marcus offered, waving his wing over the surrounding area. And without waiting for Ralph to reply, the two crows spread their wings and glided to the uppermost branches of a nearby tree.

Although he wanted to keep moving, Ralph had to admit that what Marcus had said made sense. So he dropped his backpack at his feet, and spread his blanket out on the damp grass at the water's edge.

I'll be on my way first thing tomorrow morning, Ralph thought, and then fell sound asleep.

Chapter Four
Ralph Makes a Friend

RALPH WAS DREAMING that he was at home on his lily pad, listening to the happy sounds of his children and their friends playing in the yard.

"Hey throw that water lily over here!"

"Ok, catch."

"Aw, you missed it by a mile!"

"No, that was a lousy throw."

Their laughter and playful shouting seemed to get louder, and Ralph opened one eye to watch them. But what he saw made both his eyes pop wide open in disbelief. The dream sounds he thought were those of froglets playing in the morning sun were actually the cackles of dozens of crows involved in various activities on the grass. Two of them were busy pecking at a red canvas item with two straps attached to it. Coming fully awake, he realized that it was his backpack. The crows must have carried it off while he was sleeping.

"Hey," he shouted as he hopped frantically toward them, "that's mine. Leave it alone." One of them lifted his head, cackled at Ralph and continued jabbing at the backpack. Then Ralph noticed that the other items in his backpack were strewn all over the grass.

A few feet away, a female crow, wearing Ralph's sunglasses, strutted back and forth in front of her boyfriend.

"Daryl, do you think I look like Joan Crowford, the movie star? she asked, tossing her head as the sun glinted off of the silver frames.

"You bet, gorgeous," he answered.

Ralph was about to ask for his glasses back when girlish giggling drew his attention to three more crows. Two of them stood watching the third one put the finishing touches on a hopscotch board she had drawn on an area of dry mud. Squeezing a thin line of lotion from the tip of a plastic bottle she held in her beak, she wrote a number in the center of each of the board's squares. Just as the busy bird completed a backwards 9, the lines trailed off to nothing. The bottle was empty. Ralph didn't have to guess what she had used for her numbering… it was his moisturizer.

"I don't have time for this nonsense," Ralph grumbled as he turned this way and that looking for his belongings. The crows' antics were delaying the early departure he had planned so he could continue his trip. Ralph was about to explain this to the birds when he saw another crow standing on a bit of navy blue fabric laying in a dusty heap next to the hopscotch board. It was pecking repeatedly at a round shiny object attached to it. A second object, identical to the first, lay glistening in the center of one of the hopscotch squares. Ralph recognized the shiny objects as the gold buttons from his jacket.

"Oh no," he croaked, hopping toward her, "What have you done to my jacket? Give it back to me!"

He reached for it, but the bird took off into the air with the jacket dangling from its beak. She swooped low over Ralph's head and headed for a group of crows talking on the grass nearby.

"Girls, look what I've got! It belongs to that frog guy over there. How about we use it for a game of *keep away* ?" the bird cried. Instantly, they formed a circle, and Rita, as Ralph heard her friends call her, dropped the jacket into the center of it. He moved as fast as he could to grab it, but Ralph's speed was no match for that of the crows'. Just as he got within reach of it, Rita dove into the center of the circle, snatched up the jacket and dropped it into the open beak of one of her friends.

"Your turn, Lydia," she cawed.

Back and forth, Ralph's jacket was tossed, just over his head, from one bird to another. After six or seven passes, he noticed the envelope with the payment for the team shirts fall to the ground. If the crows tore it open and scattered the bags of flies like they had done with his other belongings, it would wind up in pieces all over the cove.

Panicking at the thought, Ralph forgot about his jacket and took several huge leaps toward the envelope. But Rita reached it first. She had it in her beak and was just about to fly away with it when Ralph heard the loud flapping of wings behind him.

An angry voice shouted, "Hey Rita, don't you have anything better to do? Why don't you and your buddies go play with somethin' else? Drop the package *now*."

"Aw, Marcus, we were just havin' some fun with this guy and his stuff," Rita said, releasing the envelope from her beak.

"That's more like it," Marcus said. "Now you and your friends go pick up everything you took from our guest here and bring it back - *fast*."

Rita knew better than to argue with Marcus. With the other crows behind her, they flew off to get Ralph's things. Then Marcus turned to his small companion.

"Maurice, go after them and make sure those girls do what I said. And don't let them come back until they've got everything, understand?"

"Yes, sir," Maurice stammered, "right away, sir," and took off after them.

Watching Marcus snap out orders, Ralph was able to take his first good look at Crow Cove's leader. In the darkness the night before, he had not been able to see his host clearly. Marcus was huge, with piercing black eyes shaded by lids that were creased into a permanent frown. Around his thick neck hung a woven straw necklace from which a shiny gold charm shaped like a pair of wings dangled. Marcus considered the charm a sym-bol of his leadership. When he puffed out his chest, it glittered in the sunlight like a warning signal. And when he spread his wings, Marcus towered over the other crows, and Ralph understood why the huge bird was feared and obeyed.

Ralph had caught his breath by this time, and said, "Thank you, Marcus, for stepping in when you did." He was relieved that the crows' mischievous antics had been put to an end.

Rita and the girls, with Maurice trailing behind them, returned with Ralph's belongings, and he was ready to be on his way.

"I'll be leaving now. You've been very kind to let me stay the night," he said, stuffing the payment envelope and his crumpled jacket into his backpack.

"No problem, Ralph. You're an okay frog," Marcus said as he walked him to the stream.

"Well, so long, and thanks again," Ralph said. He slipped his arms through the backpack's tattered shoulder straps and jumped into the water.

He had been swimming for just a few seconds when he heard shrieking from the water's edge. Looking back, he saw Marcus hopping around, frantically flapping his wings and shouting for Maurice.

"Maurice," Ralph heard him yell, "get over here now. My necklace broke and the charm fell into the water. Jump in there and find it. Quick, before it sinks in the mud."

It was clear to Ralph that Marcus considered the charm more than a shiny trinket. It was his symbol of power and might be lost forever. To the leader of Crow Cove, losing the charm meant losing that power.

Ralph paused, waiting for Maurice to obey Marcus' order. When he hesitated, Marcus repeated the command, but Maurice just stood there, shaking.

"What's wrong with you? I told you to do something. Why aren't you doing it?" Marcus shouted in Maurice's face.

"Marcus, I can't go into that mud. I won't be able to breathe. I might drown," the small crow whined. "It's only a piece of scratched gold. What's the big deal, anyway?"

Fear must have been the cause of Maurice's thoughtless outburst. At any other time, Marcus would have punished the cowardly crow right on the spot, but now he was only concerned with getting his charm back. For the moment, anyway, Maurice was spared the big bird's anger.

"I'll deal with you later. Get away from me," Marcus snarled, flapping his huge wing at the frightened crow. Head down, Maurice took to the sky and flew out of sight.

Ralph watched as Marcus continued his frantic hopping, and knew he couldn't turn his back on the panicked bird. Moving around in mud was what Ralph's body was designed for, and his keen eyesight would help him locate the charm quickly. Without hesitating, Ralph swam back to the spot where the charm had fallen. He ducked his head into the mud below the water's surface and began searching.

Marcus was surprised by Ralph's sudden return and his plunge into the stream. He watched, open-beaked, as Ralph disappeared for what seemed like forever. But it was only a few seconds later when Ralph hopped out of the water onto the grass. He held out his hand with the mud-covered charm in it.

"Here you are, Marcus. Muddy, but otherwise fine. No harm done," he said.

By this time, the noisy activity at the water's edge had drawn a crowd of crows. Watching the events that had just taken place, they wondered what Marcus's reaction would be to the small frog who had saved his gold wings. But Marcus was a proud bird. Although greatly touched by Ralph's actions, Marcus just stared at him in silence. The leader of the inhabitants of Crow Cove was not able to humble himself by thanking Ralph in front of them.

Instead, he took the charm from Ralph's outstretched hand and said, "I knew I was right to let you spend the night on Crow Cove. You're an okay frog, Ralph Ribbit, you're an okay frog."

Chapter Five

Delilah Travis Gets Her Nails Done

FRIDAY MORNING WAS the busiest day of the week at *The Webbed Foot*. It was only 10 am, and the place was already jumping with customers. Many of the female frogs in the neighborhood came into the salon to get webbicures in preparation for their weekend social activities. As the manager, Ramona spent most of her time hopping around the shop making sure things ran smoothly. But it was so busy that day, she decided to do a few webbicures herself. She was almost finished applying a second coat of *Coral Reef* nail polish to Dewey Travis's wife's toes when Delilah Travis brought up the subject of Ralph's trip to *Leaps and Bounds*.

"Ramona," she began, "Dewey told me he spoke to Ralph when he passed by our pad yesterday. He said he was on his way to pick up the kids' shirts for the track meet tomorrow."

"That's right, Delilah. Coach Stone couldn't make the trip himself, so Ralph offered to go," she said, not looking up.

"Well, I don't understand why Coach just didn't ask my Dewey to go. You know how much Coach relies on him to help out with the team," she said, raising one painted foot to check out Ramona's work.

" Ralph mentioned that he wasn't sure about how to get there, and Dewey told him that he knew the way well. Ralph asked Dewey to go with him, but he's much too busy doing things around the yard, you know? Oh well. Hope Ralph will be alright on his own. Have you heard from him yet?"

In fact, Ramona had not heard from her husband, but she was not surprised. He had been gone less than a day, and didn't think Ralph had had enough time to reach the sports store. She guessed that he would wait until he had picked up the shirts and was about to start the trip back home before he sent word to his wife.

"Not yet, Delilah, but I'm sure he's fine and will let me know where he is if he gets a chance," she said.

"Oh Ramona," Delilah leaned forward in her chair and cooed, "you're so wonderfully calm. I wish I were more like you. I'd be a nervous wreck if my Dewey were in Ralph's place. I couldn't sleep at night thinking about what might happen."

If her words had alarmed Ramona, she was not about to let Delilah see it. "Ralph's a smart frog, Delilah, and I know he can handle whatever situations might come up," Ramona said. "I'm sure of it."

Relieved that she had finished Delilah's webbicure, she screwed the cap back onto the bottle of polish, stood up and said, "Okay, Delilah, you're all set. Thanks for coming in."

"Sure, dear. See you tomorrow," Delilah said. "You *do* know the meet starts exactly at noon, don't you? I just hope Ralph gets back with the shirts in time. What a shame Coach didn't ask Dewey to go for them. I guess now all we can do is hope for the best." She hopped toward the door. Biting her tongue so she wouldn't say something she would regret later, Ramona opened the door and fought a strong urge to push her out with her own polished foot.

Busy as she was at work, Ramona made sure she left the shop by a quarter to three to pick up Reggie and Roxie at school. Ramona had to get Reggie to a three o'clock appointment with Dr. Ogle, the local frogtometrist. Few frogs had weak vision, but Reggie had been complaining that he couldn't see the greenboard in school. So Ramona wasted no time in making the appointment to have Reggie's eyes checked.

She made her way to the athletic field, which sat directly behind the school building. As she got closer, Ramona saw that track practice had not yet ended. A few of the team mothers stood near the bleachers in a small group, chatting as they waited for their sons. Waving hello as she approached them, Ramona noticed Delilah Travis in the center of the small circle of moms, boasting about her son.

"Just look at my Eddy," she gloated. "He's such a talented athlete. He can jump higher and run faster than any boy on the team. I'm sure we'll win the meet tomorrow with him on the team. He's a shoo-in for the Most Valuable Player, don't you think?" Delilah chirped. None of the moms answered.

Ramona reached the group just as Delilah had finished speaking and had overheard what she said.

"Seems to me that they're all working hard for the team, Delilah, which makes each one of them a valuable player. Don't you agree?" Ramona said. Every mom in the group, except one, nodded her head in agreement. Delilah Travis just glared at Ramona and turned away.

When practice ended, everyone said their good byes and hopped off in separate directions with their children. Ramona steered Reggie in the direction of the hopscotch boards to get his sister, and they made their way to Dr. Ogle's office.

"Do you think Dad got the shirts yet, Mom?" Reggie asked.

" I don't know, Reg. *Leaps and Bounds* is a long way off. And Dad couldn't find the directions that Coach Stone gave him, so he has to figure out how to get there and back without them," Ramona explained.

"Gee, do you think he'll make it back here in time for the meet?" Reggie asked.

Ramona patted her son's shoulder. "One way or another, your father will get those shirts here. Don't you worry, son."

But Reggie was worried. He looked away so that his mother

wouldn't see his face at her mention of the missing directions.

The three of them walked in silence until they reached their destination. As they entered the waiting room, Dr. Ogle stepped out of his office to greet them.

"Come right in," he said to Reggie, "Let's have a look at those eyes."

Chapter Six

Ralph and the Rattlesnakes

THREE O'CLOCK, **RALPH** thought to himself as he glanced at the sun's position in the sky. *Four hours since I left Crow Cove.* He had been swimming ever since he left Marcus and the others late that morning, and felt he had made good progress. He wasn't sure how much further he had to travel before he reached *Leaps and Bounds*, but he was glad the stream had been easy to follow.

To show Ralph his gratitude for finding his gold charm in the mud, Marcus left Crow Cove with him, gliding low in the sky for some distance, to guide Ralph's way. The large crow knew these waters well, and led Ralph in the right direction when he had reached a fork in the stream. Satisfied that Ralph was on track, Marcus dipped his wing and cawed goodbye as he circled away and headed back toward home. Ralph felt a pang of sadness as Marcus flew into the sky and out of sight. The sudden feeling of loneliness that stabbed at his heart made him realize how much he missed his wife and kids.

Ralph swam until evening, when he stopped to rest and to check his backpack. He jumped out of the water onto the bank near a wooded area. Sliding the pack off his shoulders, he set it on the small stones and leaves at the water's edge. As Ralph turned the bag over in his hands, he was discouraged to see its condition. The crows had damaged it during their game of *keep away*. One strap was still firmly attached to the bag, but the other was badly frayed at the edges. It was held in place by only a few loose threads. Small holes and jagged tears covered the red canvas surface, and Ralph was afraid something inside might have fallen out while he was swimming.

He unzipped the bag, reached into it and began pulling its contents out. His sunglasses were still there, but the lenses were scratched. The bottle of moisturizer was gone, of course, because one of the crows had used the lotion to draw the hopscotch board.

That's alright, he told himself. *I can manage without it.*

He found the snack packs that Ramona had prepared for him, and was glad that the mischievous crows had not used them as part of their play. Ralph put one of the packs aside, planning to eat its contents as soon as he had finished checking the bag.

He pulled out his dirty jacket, now without buttons, and yanked it open to check for the payment envelope. He breathed a sigh of relief to find it still tucked safely in the pocket. But relief quickly turned to anxiety when he looked at the envelope. It too had been damaged by crows' beaks. In addition to many small holes, a tear along one side was large enough to allow some of the packets of dried flies to have fallen out, unnoticed, onto the grass at Crow Cove.

Ralph reached back into the bag for his blanket so he could lay each packet on it as he counted them. But the blanket was not there. Ralph couldn't figure out what had happened to it, until he suddenly remembered: he had used it to sleep on the night before at Crow Cove. With everything that had gone on that morning, he'd forgotten to put it back into his bag. So he placed the packets on the ground beside him.

"Eighty-three, eighty-four, eighty-five," Ralph said, dropping the last one on top of the pile. "Thank goodness, they're all here."

Ralph patched the envelope's holes and the tear with mud and put all of the packets back inside. Then he put the envelope back into his jacket pocket and replaced everything except the snack bag of grasshoppers and gnats. He was starving. Ralph usually caught his meals live on his outstretched tongue. But he didn't want to take the time waiting for his dinner to fly by. The bag of dried insects was good enough for now.

There was little light left as Ralph zipped the worn backpack and slipped it back onto his shoulders. Ralph listened to the sounds around him. Crickets chirped. Leaves whispered in the trees. Water gurgled as it slid over rocks and pebbles in the stream. They blended together in a comforting lullaby that made Ralph wish he could stay where he was and enjoy Mother Nature's music.

Then suddenly, he heard another sound, one that disrupted the soothing music of the approaching night. Rattling was coming from somewhere in the wooded area behind him. He turned around to look. Two pairs of glowing eyes stared at him from the foot of a tree. Two forked tongues shot out of open mouths. Ralph didn't move, frozen by fear. He had seen creatures like these before. They were rattlesnakes, and they were creeping right toward him.

Chapter Seven
Reggie's New Look

COMING OUT OF Dr. Ogle's office into the fading sunlight, Reggie turned to Ramona and said, "I look dorky wearing these things. All the kids are going to make fun of me."

Reggie's big round eyes looked even larger through the lenses of his new glasses. Ramona had guessed correctly that her son might need them as he struggled to read the eye chart tacked to the wall in Dr. Ogle's office. After his exam, the frogtometrist had led Reggie to the back of the room where a display case of frames stood. They came in many shapes and colors, but Reggie didn't like any of them. He peered unhappily into the case, knowing that Ramona would not let him leave without choosing a pair. Reggie finally selected round green frames that closely matched the color of his skin, hoping they would be less noticeable.

"Honey, I know you don't want to wear them, but you need to be able to see clearly," Ramona tried to reason with him, "and besides, they really look very nice on you. If the other kids notice them and make comments, it's just because they're not used to seeing a frog with glasses. You'll have something none of them have. That makes you special, doesn't it?"

"Yeah, it makes me special all right. I might as well have two heads. Just wait 'til Dewey Travis sees them. Do I have to wear them to the team picnic tonight?"

"Yes, dear, you do. There's a first time for everything, so you might as well get it out of the way now."

Reggie stuck his hands in his pockets and kicked the dirt under his feet, but didn't argue with his mother. He guessed she was right anyway.

Each year, Coach Stone had a cook-out for the kids on the track team on the lawn of his lily pad. He felt that giving them a chance to relax and have fun off the track was a good way to build team spirit that would carry over onto the track.

As planned, Ramona dropped Reggie off at Coach's on the way home from the eye doctor. When they reached his lily pad, Reggie saw that most of the kids were already there. Some were just hopping around; some were sprinting across the grass; others were practicing their jumps and shouting words of advice and encouragement to each other. Green and white striped lawn chairs sat under yellow cloth-covered picnic tables all around the yard. Smoke curled up from a large grill, and the aroma of barbequed insects filled the air.

Coach Stone saw Reggie and called out to him, "Hey Ribbit, glad you could make it. I was just going to round up the guys to come eat."

"Hi Coach. Sorry I'm late. I just came from a doctor's appointment," Reggie said.

"Yeah, your mom told me she was taking you to the frogtometrist today. Needed glasses, huh? Well, you know, they look good on you, kid," Coach said as he flipped several barbequed grasshoppers from the grill onto waiting buns.

"Come and get 'em while they're hot," he called to the kids on the lawn, waving a spatula in the air.

Reggie went over to one of the picnic tables and sat down. He drummed his fingers on the tablecloth, waiting for his teammates to notice his glasses. He knew that most of the kids would not tease him, but there were a couple who enjoyed poking fun at others. Eddy Travis was one of them. And he had just spotted Reggie.

"Hey, look who's here. It's Froggie Four Eyes," Eddy chirped. Laughing, he pointed at Reggie's glasses as the rest of the team came up behind him. Riley Schneider, Eddy's best friend, joined in the teasing.

"Whoa! Where'd you get those, Ribbit? Looks like you've got the bottom of two soda bottles on your face. You're s'posed to drink out of them, not wear them," Riley cackled.

Reggie said nothing, remembering a talk his dad had had with him about frogs like Eddy and Riley.

"Guys like that," he'd said, "do it because they get a kick out of it. The more they see that it bothers you, the more they do it. The best way to stop it is to ignore them," his dad said. Reggie believed him, but what Ralph hadn't told him was how hard it would be to do.

When Eddy noticed that his comments seemed to have no effect on Reggie, he tried again.

"Hey, Ribbit, does your dad have four eyes too? Maybe if he did, it would help him get to *Leaps and Bounds* faster." Still no reaction from Reggie. So Eddy poked him some more.

" My dad coulda made that trip in way less time than it'll take your old dad. My dad's in shape. Your dad sits around in a lab all day and plays with bugs." Eddy and Riley were bent over laughing.

Behind them, a couple of the other guys snickered, but most were silent, waiting to see what Reggie would do.

"Right, Eddy. Whatever." Reggie stood up and walked toward the grill. He had a hard time pretending to ignore the insults about his father, but the shocked look on Eddy's face made it a little easier.

"Hey Coach," he shouted, "how about a couple of grasshopper burgers?"

Coach handed Reggie a plate and said, "So what was going on over there? You guys having a good time? I heard a lot of laughing."

"Sure Coach," Reggie fibbed, "everything's great. Thanks."

He sat down at the nearest table and began to eat. The rest of the team had lined up at the grill to get their burgers, chattering about the meet. Reggie hoped that Eddy and Riley had lost interest in teasing him, but when he saw them walking toward him again, he knew there was more to come.

"So Ribbit," Eddy said, "think you'll be able to find your way to the track tomorrow with those glasses, or are you going to wind up doing your long jump down the sixth grade hall?"

"Yeah," Riley snickered, "maybe he'll break a record jumping so far that he'll hit the door of the boys' bathroom at the other end."

Scratching his head, pretending to think, he added, "Gee, I wonder if that would count?"

Reggie swallowed the last bite of his grasshopper burger, licked his fingers and stood up to face Riley. "Good question, Schneider. Why don't you ask Coach, and let me know tomorrow.

"I'm going home. I want to get plenty of rest so I can jump right through that door. Just in case it does count," Reggie said. He brushed past Riley and headed toward the edge of Coach's yard.

Reggie did not look back, so he didn't notice that Kenny

Little was following him. Kenny was the smallest member of the track team. He worked hard, but his size kept him from being one of its top athletes. But that didn't seem to bother Kenny. His big heart made up for his small size.

"Reggie, wait up," Kenny called out.

Reggie turned around. "Hi, Kenny. Didn't know you were behind me."

"Hey Reggie, I just wanted to tell you how awesome it was the way you handled Eddy and Riley. They pick on me every chance they get. I never know what to do, so I just stand there and take it."

And then, chuckling, Kenny added, "You should have seen the look on Schneider's face when you walked away from him just now."

Reggie smiled, silently thanking his father. "You can't let guys like that see that what they say bothers you. Otherwise, they just keep on doin' it, Kenny."

A look of surprise crossed Kenny's face. "You mean all those things they said didn't bother you?"

"Sure they did, especially the stuff about my dad. But he told me that it's no fun for them if you don't get upset. So I purposely acted like I didn't care. It was hard, man, because I really wanted to punch both of them in their snotty noses."

Kenny was silent for a minute and then said, "Ribbit,

glasses or no glasses, you are the coolest guy on this team. Thanks for the advice. See you tomorrow."

"No problem, Kenny. See you tomorrow," Reggie said, and hopped away toward home.

Chapter Eight
Ralph Gets Caught in the Middle

RALPH WATCHED, WIDE-EYED and afraid to move, as the two snakes crept toward him from the base of the tree. Their movements made two wavy paths through the dried leaves and twigs that covered the forest floor. When they reached Ralph, they sat on either side of him and continued to rattle their tails.

"Well, well, well, and what have we here at the edge of my forest?" one said.

"Looks like a frog to me, Jeremy," replied the other, "and it's at the edge of *our* forest."

Jeremy sighed, "Of course it's a frog, Ira. You needn't tell me what is obvious to anyone with eyes."

"Then why'd you ask me the question?"

"Ira, it was not the kind of question that needed an answer. In any case, it's not important right now."

"You don't think anything I say is important. Like about how these woods belong to both of us."

Jeremy ignored his brother's complaint and turned to Ralph, "What is your name, my good friend?"

"Ralph Ribbit, sir," he said.

"Ahhh, Mr. Ribbit. So nice to meet you. As you must have guessed, this is my younger brother Ira, and I am Jeremy. What is it that brings you to *our* part of these woods?" he said, nodding at Ira.

"I stopped here to rest on my way upstream on business," Ralph said. "I'm not familiar with this area and didn't know that these woods belong to you. I was gathering my things so I could continue my trip when I heard you and your brother talking."

Ralph's explanation did not seem to satisfy Jeremy.

"And just what is this business to which you refer? And where, may I ask, is it located?"

Ralph thought it was none of Jeremy's was business, but since he had accidentally trespassed again, he answered the snake's questions.

Ira had been silent until Ralph used the word *meet* in his explanation. Suddenly, with a puzzled look on his face, Ira said, "Meat? What do shirts have to do with meat? Are they going to wear them while they eat?"

Ralph smiled at the younger snake's confusion, but Jeremy just rolled his eyes and sighed again.

"No, no, Ira," Ralph said patiently, "not the kind of meat you eat. A meet is a contest between two teams to see which one is better. Each team wears its own special shirt so whoever watches the contest can tell the teams apart."

As soon as Ira heard the word *contest*, he cried, "Ohh! I love contests. Hey Jeremy, you and I should have a contest."

Ira looked at Ralph, "Jeremy thinks because he's the older one he should get a bigger part of these woods than me. I don't think that's fair, do you, Ralph Ribbit?"

Annoyed that his brother was inviting a stranger into their private argument, Jeremy shot him a look that would have withered a flower in full bloom.

"Ira, please," Jeremy said, "It is neither necessary nor polite to bother Mr. Ribbit with our family squabbles. How many times must I remind you that as the older brother it makes perfect sense that I be the one who gets the larger portion of this forest?"

Jeremy paused before he added, "And, in case you didn't know, dear brother, a contest requires a judge. It is his job to make a fair decision about who wins. We have no snakes here that have any wish to be fair."

When he got the chance to speak, Ralph said, "Jeremy, Ira, please excuse me but I must leave right now. There are a lot of frogs depending on me to get those shirts to them by tomorrow, and I'm already behind schedule. I'm sure that the two of you will find a fair way to work out your problem."

Jeremy was relieved to see that Ralph had no more of a wish to get involved in their business than he had, and slid backward to let him pass. But Ira was excited by the idea of a contest, and he wanted Ralph to tell them more about it.

"Maybe he could even be the fair judge we need," Ira thought. Jeremy had been right about the other snakes in the woods. None of them could be trusted. In fact, there were times when Ira wasn't sure he could even trust his own brother.

Ralph had just hopped into the water when he heard Ira call out to him, "Wait, Ralph Ribbit, wait!" Ralph turned back to look as the rattlesnake slithered through the grass toward him.

"What is it, Ira? I really need to be on my way," Ralph said.

"Oh, please don't leave just yet, Ralph Ribbit. I've just figured out who can help us solve our problem." Ira's tail rattled with excitement.

"Well, I'm very happy for you," said Ralph, "but what does that have to do with me?"

Jeremy, having heard Ira shout to Ralph, joined his brother at the edge of the stream and said, "Ira, for heaven's sake, what are you talking about? You are holding up Mr. Ribbit."

Ira ignored him and went on. "I know who will make the perfect judge, Jeremy. And he's right here."

Jeremy cast a doubtful look at Ira and said, "And just who might that be?"

"Why Ralph Ribbit, Jeremy, Ralph Ribbit!"

Chapter Nine
Ralph Solves a Problem

RALPH'S JAW DROPPED. He stared at Ira, not believing what he'd just heard. The last thing he needed now was to have to judge a contest between two rattlesnakes. He had no time and no wish to choose the winner.

He shook his head and said, "Ira, I can't possibly stay. I would like to help you out, but I just can't spare the time right now. I'm sorry, but you will just have to find some other way to divide this forest between you and your brother."

"We've tried to do that lots of times before, but Jeremy always wants to do everything his way. And he won't even listen to my ideas. I was really hoping you could help us, Ralph Ribbit," Ira said, hanging his head.

Jeremy slid over to his brother and said, "Come, come, Ira. Mr. Ribbit said he has to leave in order to complete his business on time. Surely you can understand that." He turned from his younger brother and looked at Ralph, "Mr. Ribbit, you must understand that Ira is an adult with the heart and spirit of a child. He wants what he wants when he wants it, and he pouts on those occasions when he does not get what he wants. Please ignore his pleading, and don't let it keep you from continuing on your journey. Good luck to you, sir." And as smoothly as he had moved to join Ralph, he slid back toward the woods, rattling his tail for his brother to follow him.

Ralph watched Ira trailing behind Jeremy, head down and rattle silent. As he slowly wound away from him, Ralph thought about his own children when they were hurt or disappointed. His heart ached for Ira and once again, he knew that he could not just walk away from the unhappy snake. Rubbing his chin, he thought about how he could help Ira and Jeremy solve their problem. Ralph thought and thought, and finally had an idea.

"Ira, Jeremy, wait!" Ralph called to them. "I may be able to help you after all."

At the sound of his voice, the two brothers looked back at Ralph in surprise. "Really, Ralph Ribbit, really? You thought of a contest for us? And you'll be the judge?"

Ralph smiled at Ira. "Not really a contest Ira. But I do have an idea that will let you and your brother work together to solve your problem."

"Ohhh! What is it? What is it? Will it be fun? Tell us, Ralph Ribbit." Ira was bubbling over with excitement.

Jeremy, however, did not share his brother's enthusiasm.

"Really, Mr. Ribbit. You are most kind to put our needs ahead of your own, and we do appreciate your offer to help us. But I must insist that you leave immediately as you planned. I assure you that my brother and I can work things out between us. Isn't that right, Ira?"

"No Jeremy, we can't. I want to hear his idea. I bet it's a good one, too," Ira said, wiggling around on the grass. "Tell us what it is, Ralph Ribbit!"

Ralph looked at Jeremy and said, "If it's alright with you, the solution to your problem is pretty simple. I've done this with my own children when they fight over how to divide up something they both want."

"Like what? Like what?" Ira cried.

"Like the last slice of Black Fly pie," Ralph said, smiling at the thought. "If you truly want a fair way to split up this forest, this is the best way I know to do that."

But Jeremy didn't care about being fair. He had always felt that because he was older, he should make the final decision about how the forest would be divided. However, now that Ira had brought Ralph into their business, Jeremy felt forced to go along. Nodding his head at Ralph he said reluctantly, "Of course, Mr. Ribbit. Do go on."

"Well, we'll need a few things before we get started. Let's go back to the forest, and on our way, Ira, would you gather a good supply of stones and pile them up right here?" Ralph pointed to a place on the ground that bordered the entrance to the woods.

"Okay, Ralph Ribbit. That's easy. What are we going to do with them?" Ira asked as he scooted back and forth, pushing rocks into a heap at the spot Ralph had pointed out.

"Be patient, Ira. You'll see how we're going to use them very soon," he replied.

Jeremy sat silent, watching and worrying.

It took Ira only a few minutes to do as Ralph had asked.

"Ok, Ralph Ribbit. Here they are. Now what?"

Ralph stood between the two snakes and said, "You both must understand that this can only work if each of you does his part. If not, then we all will have wasted our time, and for nothing. Are you both willing to do that?"

Ira bobbed his head up and down. Jeremy, who was not at all happy, merely nodded his head.

"Jeremy," Ralph said, "you will have your turn first."

The corner of Jeremy's mouth turned upward in a smirk. *Maybe this won't be so bad after all,* he thought.

"Then Ira will take his turn."

Now it was Ira who was not happy. His eyes glowed red and he flicked his tongue at Ralph.

"Why does he always get to go first? Just because he's older," Ira complained. "This plan is no different than any of the ones Jeremy makes up."

"Ira," Ralph said, "please let me finish."

"Yes, Ira, do be quiet and let Mr. Ribbit continue," Jeremy said, bowing to Ralph.

"Jeremy," Ralph said, "you will divide the forest into two sections by making a line across it with the rocks. The area on one side of the line will be yours, and the area on the other side will be your brother's."

"*What?*" Ira screeched as his brother slid toward the rock pile. "That's not fair at all. Jeremy will divide the forest so that he has the bigger section. I don't like this plan, Ralph Ribbit. I thought this was supposed to be fair. And now, not only does Jeremy get his turn first, but he gets to decide where the dividing line is. I wish I never asked you to help us!"

Ralph said, "Hold on, Ira. Stay with me for just a few more minutes, okay? I promise you that my plan is fair. You must trust me."

"Yeah, right," Ira said, turning toward his brother, who was busy sliding rocks into a line that already stretched half way across the forest.

"Look! Look where he made the dividing line. It's nowhere

near the middle. He made his side bigger than mine, just like he always does. I told you so, Ralph Ribbit!"

Ralph did not answer as he watched Jeremy finish the rock line that split the woods in two. One side was clearly bigger than the other. Jeremy slithered back to Ralph and grinned at Ira.

"Good, Jeremy. You've done your part. Are you sure you're satisfied with where you placed the line?" Ralph asked. "Once Ira takes his turn you cannot make any changes."

Jeremy was quick to answer. "Why certainly I'm satisfied, Mr. Ribbit."

"Fine. Now then, it's Ira's turn to do his part," Ralph said as he turned to Ira. "Are you ready?"

"I guess so, I don't even care anymore. This is so not fair," Ira sulked, looking at the ground. "What do I have to do?"

Ralph pointed to the rocks that Jeremy had not used. "Ira, each section of the woods needs to be labeled. Your job is to use those rocks to write your name in the section you want and your brother's name in the other. Since Jeremy chose where to draw the line, it's only fair that you get first choice of the section you want for yourself."

Neither brother moved for a few seconds, trying to understand what Ralph had just said.

Jeremy was the first to realize what was happening.

"Now wait just a moment, Mr. Ribbit," he sputtered. "You

clearly said that I was the one to draw the line that divided the forest."

"Yes, Jeremy, I did," Ralph said, "but I didn't say anything about choosing which section would be yours. That decision is Ira's. That's fair, isn't it?"

Jeremy was silent. Ralph had outsmarted him. Or maybe he had outsmarted himself. But it was too late now. Ira was going to own the larger portion of the woods, and he had handed it to him.

Well, he thought, *I'll just wait until this frog leaves us and then figure out some way to get the larger section of forest for myself.*

Ralph looked at Ira, who had not moved. "What's the matter Ira? It's your turn now. You must take it."

"I'm ashamed, Ralph Ribbit. I asked you to stay here to help us when you really needed to leave. You did, and then I yelled and was mean to you. I'm sorry I didn't believe you when you promised to be fair."

Ralph smiled and said, "That's alright, Ira. You didn't know what my plan was, and I know it looked as if I wasn't being fair. But the choice is still yours. Why don't you take some of the smaller rocks and use them to label each side of the forest with your names? Hurry though, I have to leave as soon as you're done."

Ira grinned and did his part. Once he had labeled each section, he called to Ralph and Jeremy.

"I'm all finished. Come and look! Now we finally know which section is mine and which one is Jeremy's. No more arguments!"

Ralph and Jeremy joined Ira at the edge of the forest. By this time it was dark. The only light came from the glow of the moon as it shone on the ground in front of them.

Ralph looked at the names written on either side of the rock line. "Why Ira!" Ralph said, astonished at what he saw. "You wrote Jeremy's name in the larger section! I thought you wanted it to be yours."

A small smile crossed Ira's face, " I did, Ralph Ribbit, until just now. But then I realized it was mostly because I was angry with Jeremy and didn't want him to win. Then I remembered that you did this with your own kids when they couldn't decide how to share something. You knew their feelings about each other were more important than the size of a piece of--, what kind of pie was it?"

"Black fly pie," Ralph said softly.

"Right! Black fly pie! That's it. Anyway, it made me think about how Jeremy is more important than some old forest. So I gave him the bigger part because it will make him happy. And it makes me happy too. Now we can be brothers, not enemies," Ira said.

Jeremy, who had not spoken, went over to his brother and said, "Ira, I may be older than you are, but you are wiser. In the end, family should always come first, and you were the first to learn that. It is I who should be ashamed of my be-havior these past months. Can you forgive me?"

" 'Course I can, Jeremy. Besides, it was Ralph Ribbit's plan. I just wanted us to be a family. And you know what? He was right—it all worked out for the best. It's him we should thank."

"You're right again, Ira," Jeremy said, and turned to Ralph. But he was gone.

As the two rattlesnakes sat side by side in the darkness, peer-ing at the stream, they saw the shadow of a frog waving to them as he hopped into the water and paddled away.

Chapter Ten
The Bedtime Story

RAMONA AND ROXANNE sat together under the yellow glow of the porch light hanging from the branch of a tree. They were waiting for Reggie to get back from Coach Stone's. The evening stars winked at them and a warm breeze brushed their faces. Suddenly Roxanne jumped up and pointed at a shadow bouncing along the edge of the stream.

"There he is, Mom," she said, "Reggie's coming!"

Ramona went to the edge of the lily pad to meet her son as he hopped onto the porch. Although she had hidden her feelings from Reggie, Ramona was anxious about how the guys on the track team would react to his glasses. A frog who wore glasses stood out from other frogs, and was a target for teasing and jokes.

"So, how was the picnic, Reg? Did you have a good time? What did your friends have to say about your glasses?" she asked.

"I bet they really liked them," Roxanne chirped, looking up at Reggie. "You look soooo cool and smart in them."

Reggie smiled at his sister's loyalty. She was too young to know that most sixth graders, especially boys, did not think smart was cool at all.

"It was okay," Reggie said as he sat down next to them. "Eddy and Riley were on my case about them in front of the rest of the team, but I tried to do what Dad told me to do."

"I'm proud of you, Reg. And Dad will be too when he hears about it," Ramona said.

"By the way," Reggie said, "where do you think Dad is right now? It's Friday night and the meet starts at noon tomorrow. Do you think he found the place and picked up the shirts yet?"

"I don't know, sweetie. But I can tell you that when Dad says he'll do something, he does it. Why don't you both get to bed early tonight? Tomorrow is a big day for all of us," Ramona said.

"Okay mom. Come on, Roxie," Reggie said. As he picked her up to carry her off to her room, she looked at him with tears in her eyes.

"What's wrong, sis? You don't want to go to bed?"

"I miss my daddy," she sobbed, burying her head into her brother's chest. "I wish he was here to tell me a story before I go to sleep."

Reggie felt a tug of sympathy pull at his heart. He knew how much Roxanne looked forward to the nightly story their father told her.

"Do you want me to tell you a story tonight? I know a good one," he said.

"Really Reggie?" she said giving him a small smile. "Okay. What's it about?"

"Can't tell you until you're in bed. Hurry up and get ready!"

"Okay, I'll be really quick," Roxie said, hopping out of his arms.

By the time Reggie got to her room, Roxie had changed into her pajamas and was snuggled deep in her bed, hugging her stuffed mouse. She waited for her brother to begin his story.

"I'm ready, Reggie!" she said.

"Okay, Roxie." he said, "This is a story about a very special frog..."

Once upon a time, there was a toad named Rupert. He lived with his family on a lily pad at the edge of a stream. Rupert had a wife and two children who he loved more than anything else in the world. He also had many friends. Everyone loved Rupert too, because he was kind and helpful.

Rupert worked hard at his job as a scientist at a laboratory, but he spent his time out of work with his family and friends.

One night, his daughter Ruby was getting ready for bed. She was sad because she couldn't find her favorite stuffed mouse. Rupert looked everywhere for it, but he couldn't find it either. Ruby took the toy to bed with her, and Rupert felt sorry that she would have to go to sleep without it.

He thought for a minute and then went to his sock drawer and dug out an old gray sweat sock. He rummaged through his wife's sewing basket and found a needle and thread, a soft rag and a few other small items. Rupert worked busily for almost an hour, stuffing and shaping the sock into the head and body of an animal. Then he stitched two pink felt ears, two black button eyes, a tiny gray button nose onto its head and a thin blue ribbon tail onto the end of its body.

Rupert held out the stuffed mouse he had made and said to Ruby, "Do you think you can go to sleep with this, honey?"

Ruby squealed with delight as she hugged it to her and said, "Oh yes, Daddy, I love it!" From that night on, the gray sock mouse became Ruby's favorite toy.

A few days later, Rupert's neighbor Freda sprained her foot. It hurt too much for her to walk, and she had to spend all day sitting on a chair. He thought she would be more comfortable if she could rest her foot on a stool, so Rupert spent two evenings making one out of soft leaves and grass. Freda loved it, and offered to knit him a sweater while her foot healed. But Rupert said he was just happy that the stool made her more comfortable.

Captain Nemo, another neighbor, almost drowned when rough water tipped his boat over during a storm. He was too small to get the boat right-side up by himself, so Rupert offered to help him. The water was ice cold and the wind was blowing hard, but Rupert jumped in anyway. Together, he and Captain Remo flipped the boat up again. The Captain wanted to give Rupert a new fishing pole as a thank you, but Rupert wouldn't take it.

"Just give me one of the fish you catch, if you have any extra," he said.

Then one day Rupert had an accident in his lab at work. His hands were badly burned and had to be bandaged so they could heal. With his hands tied up, there was not much Rupert could do. He was not able to go to work or do any chores around the house. He was bored and depressed. Ruby saw him sitting in his armchair, staring out the window. She remembered how she felt when she lost her stuffed toy, and how hard Rupert had worked to make her a new one. Ruby wanted to make her daddy happy, so she decided to tell him a story just like the ones he told her each night. She sat beside him on a small stool near his feet and told him about a little gray mouse. And, for the first time that week, Rupert smiled. It was the best story he had ever heard.

He was still smiling when the door opened and in walked Captain Remo and Freda. Freda told Rupert her foot was feeling much better thanks to the stool he had made for her.

She stood in front of him holding a steaming pot in her hands and said, "I asked your wife what you like to eat and she told me you like grasshopper stew. So I made this for you to cheer you up."

Rupert was about to thank her when Captain Remo placed a bucket of water containing several large trout on the floor next to him.

"Y' know, neighbor, if you hadn'ta helped me set my boat straight after that storm a while back, I'da been in big trouble. Thanks to you I can still go fishin', and I'm mighty grateful. Caught these beauties just for you."

"Freda, Captain Remo, I appreciate the thank you gifts, but I didn't expect anything in return. I just did what any good neighbor would do," he said.

And then he added, smiling for the second time that day, "Why don't you both stay for dinner? We're having grasshopper stew and fried trout!"

"The End," Reggie said as he stood up. "Well, Roxie, how did you like my story?"

Roxanne smiled and clapped her hands. "I liked it alot, Reggie. But I have one question."

"Okay, what is it?"

"Is Rupert supposed to be Daddy?"

Reggie shook his head and grinned. "You know, for a little kid, you're pretty smart. Now go to sleep. Nite, kiddo."

"Nite Reggie. See you in the morning," she said, and then called out after him, "and Daddy too!"

Chapter Eleven
Leaps and Bounds At Last

RALPH MOVED STEADILY through the water, over and between the rocks that dotted the streambed, wondering how much time had passed since he'd left Jeremy and Ira. He had been swimming in the darkness for some time, guided by the pearly light cast by the moon. Judging that it had to be near eight o'clock, Ralph was thankful that *Leaps and Bounds* stayed open until nine on Friday night. He hurried along, anxious to reach the store before it closed.

As he paddled, Ralph tried to picture the map that Coach Stone had drawn for him, hoping to recall any detail that might provide a clue as to how close he was to his destination. He wished he had looked at it more closely when Coach gave it to him, but he'd decided to wait until he got home to study it carefully. So he'd folded it and tucked it into his jacket, giving it only the briefest glance.

The stream had run a straight course since he'd waved good-bye to the happy rattlesnake brothers and hopped into the water to continue his journey. He followed it as it curved this way and that. But as he looked ahead, he saw that the stream split in two again. Another decision to make.

Why, he thought, *is it always nighttime when I reach a fork in the stream? It would be so much easier to see what's ahead of me in daylight.* But in the darkness everything was a shapeless shadow.

When Ralph reached the spot where the stream divided, he saw small bushes and reeds growing out of a large mound of earth. A rock jutting out of it gave him a place to stop and look at his surroundings. Hopping onto it, he looked down the ribbon of water that curled to his left, but saw nothing. Then he looked to his right. A blinking light some distance away reflected off the leaves of the nearby trees.

Where is that light coming from? he wondered. Common sense told Ralph to head toward it, so he plunged back into the water and paddled in that direction. With each stroke, the light grew brighter. And then he saw it: a large structure on the left bank with hundreds of lightning bugs flickering across its roof in letters that spelled *L-E-A-P-S & B-O-U-N-D-S.*

"Finally! I made it," he exclaimed, "and it's still open!" Ralph jumped onto the bank and hurried into the store.

The lighted sign on the roof was just an inviting wink compared to the lightning bug spotlights that stared down, white-hot, at the store's merchandise. Woven reed and grass shelves were packed with shirts, sweat pants, socks and shorts. Each of a dozen tables displayed a variety of items such as golf balls, tee shirts, tennis rackets, baseballs, catcher's mitts and water bottles. Shoe boxes containing sneakers, cleats and moccasins sat, one on top of the other, along the back wall.

When Ralph's eyes adjusted to the sudden brightness, he looked around for someone to help him. He was surprised that there were so many other customers in the store at that hour. Three of them stood at the checkout counter. Four more wandered from table to table, picking through the items on them.

Ralph recognized the sales toads by the navy blue golf shirts they wore. The shirts each had a green frog leaping toward a yellow "L&B" sewn onto the pocket. But because they were all busy with other customers, none of the sales clerks noticed him.

As Ralph walked up to the checkout counter and stood at the end of the line, the overhead lights began to blink on and off: a sign that the store would be closing for the night.

Surely they won't turn me out before I get the shirts, he thought.

By the time he reached the front of the line, the doors had been locked. Ralph shifted his weight from one foot to the other, waiting for someone to help him. Finally it was his turn.

"How may I help you, sir?" the frog behind the counter asked. A nametag pinned to his shirt identified him as Walter, the assistant manager.

"Yes, Walter, I'm here to pick up an order of track shirts for Muddyville Middle School," Ralph said.

"Okay, I'd be happy to help you with that, May I have the purchase order?" he said, holding out his hand.

Ralph stared at Walter and gasped, "Purchase order? I'm supposed to have a purchase order?"

Chapter Twelve
Another Problem for Ralph

RALPH FROZE. COACH Stone hadn't mentioned anything about a purchase order. He remembered seeing only
the bags of dried flies in the payment envelope.

"Yes, Mr. Ribbit. It's a pink sheet with a number on it that
helps us find your order," Walter said.

Ralph yanked the payment envelope from the inside pocket
of his jacket.

"Maybe it's stuck in the bottom of the envelope," he said as
he shook it. The bags of dried flies spilled onto the counter,
but no pink paper came with them. Then he looked into the
envelope, but it was empty.

Ralph rested his elbows on the counter and put his head in
his hands. His words were muffled as he spoke through his
fingers.

"Can you think of any other way to find the shirts without
the purchase order? I must have them tonight," he pleaded.

"I'll be letting my son and his team down if they don't have them for the meet tomorrow."

Ralph lifted his face to look at Walter, who saw his discouraged look.

"I'm really sorry sir," he said, "but the orders are filed by number, not by name. Without the number on the purchase order, I have no way of knowing where to look for the shirts."

"Well, I don't seem to have it," he said miserably. And then he had a sickening thought. Had the purchase order been in the envelope when the birds on Crow Cove played *keep away* with his backpack? Had it fallen out during their game? Since Coach had not mentioned that it was in there, Ralph did not miss it when he gathered the bags of flies before he left the Cove. It seemed like a logical explanation, but it didn't change anything. He still didn't have the paper.

"Is there any other way you can locate the shirts for me? I'm a long way from home and I have to travel all night to get back with them in time for the meet," Ralph said.

Walter didn't think there was anything he could do at that hour, but he knew there was someone who might be able to help the desperate frog.

"Wait here just a minute, sir. I'll be right back," Walter said. He headed toward the sales toads who were tidying up the jumbled items on the display tables. The last of the late shoppers were gone, and he was the only customer still in the store.

Walter whispered something to one of the sales toads, who nodded and came back to the counter with a third clerk. Their name tags identified them as Hal, the store manager, and Rocco.

"Mr. Ribbit," Hal said, extending his hand to shake Ralph's. "Walter explained your situation to me. He also mentioned that you're from Muddyville Middle School. I went there myself quite a while back. Was on the track team too. What a coincidence! Nice that the kids will have uniform shirts. Didn't have them in my years there.

"Here's the problem. Without the purchase order number, finding your shirts would be almost impossible-- like searching for a pebble in a rock pile. But they're for my old school, and I'd like the kids to have them for the meet tomorrow. As manager, I can keep the store open after its normal closing time. I'm going to let my sales clerks go back into the store room to try to find your order. Walter has offered to help and so has Rocco. Maybe between the two of them, they can find it. Any other details you can give them?"

"Of course, of course," Ralph said.

"Jack Stone ordered 25 gold shirts with *Muddyville Middle School* printed across the front in blue. I think he placed the order about six months ago. Is that any help?"

"Well, it's a start," Hal said. He started walking to the back of the store, motioning to Walter and Rocco to follow.

"Let's get on it, boys."

Not sure what to do, Ralph followed them, but Hal stopped him as they came to the storeroom door.

"Sorry, Mr. Ribbit. I can't let you back there, but you can watch from here," Hal said. He pointed to a large window cut into the wall that separated the store from the storeroom.

"I'll be in my office," he said, unlocking the door. "Good luck, boys."

Ralph peered through the glass. The storeroom was a maze of boxes of all sizes and shapes, piled almost to the ceiling. Taped to the top of each box was a slip with a purchase order number and a name written on it in black marker. Walter and Rocco started at opposite ends of the room and moved boxes as quickly as they could, looking for the name "Stone." It was back-breaking work, and after an hour, they still had not found the box.

Hal came out of his office and went over to Ralph. "I think we'll have to stop for the night, Mr. Ribbit. I've got to let these guys go home. We can start looking again first thing in the morning."

"I understand, Hal. You've gone out of your way to help me. I guess I have no choice but to wait until morning. Thanks for your time tonight," Ralph said, feeling tired and defeated.

He was about to walk away from the window when he saw Walter teetering on top of a pile of boxes near the wall. He seemed to be looking at something on the floor behind them, when suddenly he jumped off the pile and out of sight.

"What's Walter doing?" Ralph asked Hal.

"I don't know, but I'm going to find out right now," he said, opening the storeroom door.

"Walter, what's going on? What are you doing back there? It's time to go home," Hal called out. The sound of rustling paper came from behind the pile. Then Hal heard a grunt as a box sailed over the top of the pile and landed on the floor in front of him.

"Hey! Watch out! You almost hit me. Come out of there now, Walter!"

Unable to climb back over the pile of boxes that he'd jumped off of minutes earlier, Walter had found a narrow space between the rows and squeezed through it. Dusty and out of breath, he stood, grinning, in front of Hal.

"I think I found Mr. Ribbit's shirts," Walter said. "Look at this. It must've fallen behind the others."

Hal stared at the box Walter held. One of its corners was smashed and had a small tear in it. Most of the pink purchase order, which had been attached to the top, was torn off. The part that was left dangled on a thin piece of tape. All that was left of the name on the sheet were the letters "ne." The five digit order number was gone too, except for the last two-25—the number of items in the box. Through the tear in the box, a small patch of gold fabric could be seen.

"Well, whaddya know," Hal said. "We'll have to check

inside to be sure, but this seems to be the right box. Good job, Walt! Let's open it up."

Hal grabbed a letter opener from a table near the stockroom door and slit the top of the box. He pulled out the first item his hand touched and held it up in front of him. Its small size told him it was a kid's shirt, and the gold fabric with *Muddyville Middle School* stitched in blue across the front were proof that Walter had found Ralph's order.

Still holding the shirt against his chest, Hal turned toward the window and smiled at Ralph through the plate glass. The look of relief on Ralph's face made the extra hour Hal had kept the store open so that his sales toads could look for the shirts worth every minute.

Walter and Rocco were standing with Hal near the stockroom door when he opened the box. Now, grinning at them, Hal put the shirt back into the box, taped it shut and handed it to Ralph.

"Here's your order, Mr. Ribbit. You're all set."

Chapter Thirteen
The Storm

TWO HOURS AFTER he had walked into *Leaps and Bounds*, Ralph walked out carrying the bulky box of shirts. He smiled as he wiggled his fingers. They were still tingling from shaking hands with Hal, Walter and Rocco for helping him find his order.

As he waved goodbye, he thought about the trip downstream. The clear sky that had helped him find the store had become dark and starless. A black cloud now sat in front of the moon, and a cold wind whipped through the trees. Ralph stopped so he could put on his jacket.

That's better, he thought as he buttoned the only one left on it.

Shifting the position of the box in his arms, Ralph hugged it close to his chest. He bent his head against the blustery wind and hurried to the water's edge. To get back in time for the meet, he would have to travel through the night. The coming storm would make it even harder, but Ralph was not going to let a little wind and rain stop him.

Maybe if I'm lucky, the trip back will be faster than the trip here, Ralph thought.

And then... Plop. Plop. Plop. Large raindrops hit Ralph's head and made wet circles on the box. He looked up at the sky just as a jagged bolt of lightning sliced through the darkness. A clap of thunder crashed overhead as the clouds burst open and a drenching rain began. It beat down on Ralph with great force, like a torrent of rocks hurled at him by an angry Mother Nature.

The ground turned to mud, and Ralph slipped and slid with every step. He tightened his hold on the box, struggling to keep his balance. The breeze that whispered through the trees earlier that evening now roared through their branches, whipping them back and forth and slapping Ralph's face. The stream roared past him, crashing over rocks in its way. Walking was difficult, but he kept moving.

Ralph concentrated on each step he took, straining to see the ground beneath him. But when he turned his head to glance at the water, his foot hit a patch of muddy leaves. His legs came out from under him, and he tumbled into the rushing water. The force of his landing caused the box to fly out of his arms and get whisked away. The strong current slammed Ralph into rocks as it bounced him downstream. And through it all, his only thought was of the shirts.

His terrifying ride came to an end a few minutes later when he hit a large log jutting out into the water from the bank of the stream. Out of breath and badly bruised, he managed to drag himself onto it. He took his backpack from his shoulders and set it down beside him. The bumpy ride had all but destroyed it. The jagged edges of the rocks had sliced through the red canvas in a dozen places, and it was covered in mud.

As he sat on the log, Ralph noticed that the storm had begun to move away. The roar of the water had quieted to a whisper, and the wind had dwindled to a breeze. The dark clouds that covered the moon had parted, and slivers of light now glittered on the ripples in the stream.

Ralph looked around and wondered where he was. Behind him was a wooded area of trees that stood so close together they looked like a wall against the sky. He turned back to face the stream, hoping to catch a glimpse of the box of shirts, but saw nothing. He couldn't believe that he'd gone through so much to get them, only to have them ripped away by the storm.

How can I face Coach Stone and the team without those shirts? They're counting on me. And what about Reggie? I've let him down most of all, Ralph thought, pacing back and forth along the log.

He thought about swimming back toward *Leaps and Bounds* to look for the shirts, but decided against it. Whether he found them or not, by the time he reached the school, the track meet would be over.

Ralph slipped the ruined backpack over his shoulders and hopped off the log onto the grass. The stream no longer followed a straight path, but wound around the edge of the forest in a huge half-circle. Ralph knew that it would be faster if he cut through the woods rather than follow the stream around them, but he did not want to take the chance of getting lost in the forest. If he stayed near the water, he might even spot the box of shirts.

Night had lightened into dawn, making it easier for Ralph to travel. His attention was focused on the path in front of him, and he didn't notice the two crows circling above him. It wasn't until he heard a sharp "Caw, caw" that he looked up and saw the pair of birds swoop down and land right in front of him.

"Hey Ralph! We thought that was you!" the larger bird chirped.

"Marcus! And Maurice! Good to see you! How did you know it was me?" Ralph was surprised to see his two friends from Crow Cove.

"Well, we were out lookin' around to see what we could find after the storm," Maurice explained, "and we spotted some-thing movin' on that rock. When we saw a little green frog carryin' a beat up red backpack we knew it had to be you."

"Yeah," said Marcus. "We thought you'da been back home by now. How come you're still so far away---and where are the shirts?"

In a voice that quivered with emotion, Ralph explained what had happened since he'd left *Leaps and Bounds*.

"The track meet is going to start in a couple of hours, and

if I can't find the shirts, I'll have let my son and the team down. And I don't have time to go back and look for them. I'll hardly have time to get to the meet if I leave right now. I feel just terrible," Ralph said in a choked whisper.

Marcus looked at the frog that stood next to him. Ralph had gone out of his way to dig his gold charm out of the mud at the bottom of the stream when Maurice had been too frightened to do it. He had become his friend that day, and now Ralph needed help.

"Hey Maurice, listen up," Marcus said. "Go back to the Cove and find Jimmy, Max, Simon, Bobby and Merle. They're our best hunters. Tell them I need them *now* to help our friend Ralph. Bring 'em right back here with you. And make it quick. Got that?"

"I'm on my way," Maurice said, and took off into the sky.

Then Marcus turned to Ralph and said, "Ok, buddy, get moving toward your son's school."

"But what about the shirts?" Ralph asked.

"My boys and I are going to look for them. And when we find them we'll bring 'em to you," Marcus said.

Touched by the crow's kindness, Ralph said, "I'm so grateful to you for doing this for me, Marcus. How can I thank you?"

"You don't need to thank me, Ralph. We're friends. And friends help each other. Period. Now go. We'll catch up with you somewhere along the stream," Marcus said. He spread his wings to take off but then paused.

"Oh, wait a minute! I almost forgot. How many shirts are there?"

"Twenty-five," Ralph replied. "They're gold with blue letters stitched on the front."

"Got it. We'll find 'em. Don't worry," Marcus said.

Ralph watched him sail into the sky until he was no more than a black dot.

"Thank you, my friend," he called, praying that Marcus was right.

Chapter Fourteen
Ralph Takes a Shortcut

EARLY ON SATURDAY morning, Ramona sat at the edge of their lily pad catching insects for breakfast. Reggie and Roxie were still asleep, and in the quiet that surrounded her, she thought about her husband. She was not surprised that she hadn't heard from Ralph during his trip, but thought surely he would have had enough time to get to the sports store and back again by now. She hoped he was safe.

Reggie was anxious too. He had come home from the cookout at Coach's the night before, and asked Ramona how long it would be before Ralph got back with the shirts. Not wanting to worry Reggie, she told him that his father would be back soon. But it was eight o'clock and he had not returned. The meet started at noon. Time was running out.

Ramona hopped back to her kitchen with her breakfast bugs. She put half of them into each of two bowls, sprinkled them with the crushed petals of water lilies that grew nearby and set them out on the table.

"Reggie! Roxanne! Time to get up! It's a big day today," she called.

Eyes still filled with sleep, Roxie followed her brother out into the kitchen and looked around expectantly.

"Isn't daddy home yet?" she asked, sitting down in front of her breakfast bowl.

"Gee Mom, he's still not home? Where is he?" Reggie asked.

Determined to keep her own concern hidden from her children, she said firmly, "I don't know, kids. But I can tell you this. Your father knows how important it is for the team to have their shirts. He'll get back with them in time for the meet one way or another. Daddy doesn't make promises he can't keep. Finish your cereal and get washed and ready to go to the track, okay?"

As Ramona wondered where Ralph was, he was bouncing along the stream as it wound around the edge of the forest. The arrival of the crows had given him new hope. By himself, Ralph would not have been able to do what Marcus and his buddies were doing for him----re-tracing his steps from *Leaps and Bounds* to find the shirts. Now there was still a chance that he could deliver the shirts to the meet on time and keep his promise to Reggie and the team.

Ralph looked up at the sky and figured it must be almost

nine o'clock. He bounded along as quickly as he could, but circling around the woods was not only taking him out of his way, but wasting precious time as well.

As Ralph looked for signs of the cardboard box or the gold shirts, he was thinking about Ramona and the kids. They must be wondering where he was, and worrying.

Just keep moving. 'Slow and steady wins the race,' Ralph thought, remembering story of *The Tortoise and The Hare*. He often told Roxie a fairy tale at bedtime, and that was one of her favorites.

When he was half way around the forest, Ralph saw something move in the distance. As he got closer, he saw it sliding back and forth across a line of rocks that led off into the woods. And suddenly, he realized where he was. He was back at the spot where he had met Ira and Jeremy yesterday on his way to *Leaps and Bounds*. He had helped them settle an argument and had left the brothers happy and at peace with each other.

Just then the figure near the rocks lifted its head and stared at him. "Ralph Ribbit! Is it really you, Ralph Ribbit?" It was Ira, and he was scooting toward him.

"What are you doing here? Do you have your son's shirts? Did you come back to visit me and Jeremy? Can you stay for a little while?"

"Ira," Ralph said, smiling at his excited greeting. "I'm actually on my way back home, but I've run into some trouble."

The snake did not take his eyes off Ralph as he explained what had happened to him and the shirts.

"...and so I have to hop around the edge of the forest. If I cut through it and get lost in the woods, I'll have wasted the little time that I have left to get back home," he finished.

"Gee, Ralph Ribbit, that's too bad," Ira said. He wanted help his new friend and he creased his brow in thought as he listened to Ralph. Suddenly a smile brightened his face.

"Oh, but wait a minute!" Ira cried. "You don't have to go around the woods. Jeremy and I can show you a shortcut through them. That way, you'll get home faster. Let's find him, and we'll lead you right out of here," Ira said.

Ralph could not believe this lucky turn of events. For the second time that day, he had been blessed with the good fortune of meeting up with friends. And they were eager to help him.

"That would be great, Ira," Ralph said, smiling.

"No problem, Ralph Ribbit. Just follow me," the snake said.

Ira scooted into the woods and found Jeremy, who was also glad to help their new friend. Ralph hopped along behind the brothers as they wove their way through tangled bushes and hanging tree branches. Excited about the shortcut, he had completely forgotten that Marcus and the other crows expected to find him where they had left him at the stream near the edge of the forest. Ira and Jeremy led him through to the other side when Ralph finally remembered.

Oh no, he thought,*what have I done now?*

Chapter Fifteen
Where Is Ralph Ribbit?

RAMONA, REGGIE AND Roxanne hopped along the sidewalk bordering Muddyville Middle School and headed toward the athletic field. Even from a distance, they could see that it was already bustling with activity. With just two hours to go before the championship track meet began, many preparations were being made.

Several officials, wearing black and white striped shirts, were on the track, setting up equipment for the jumping, hurdle and relay events. At the far end of the field, two maintenance workers prepared an area of ground for the pole vault. Coaches from each of the three schools competing in the meet stood with their teams gathered around them giving directions or pep talks. Near the spectator stands, parents set up refreshment tables.

Reggie spotted Coach Stone and the team. Pointing to them, he said, "There they are mom. I'll see you later," and hopped away to join them.

"Good luck, Reg. We'll be cheering for you," she called.

As she and Roxie crossed the field, Ramona's eyes darted this way and that looking for Ralph. She thought he might have come directly to the school with the shirts. She looked at Reggie sitting with his teammates and Coach Stone, but did not see her husband among them.

The boys will be so disappointed if they don't have those shirts, she thought. And for the first time since Ralph had left two days before, she began to wonder if he would get back in time. She tried to ignore the stab of fear that pierced her heart.

Oh Ralph, where are you? Ramona cried silently. Her wonderings were interrupted as a shrill voice called to her.

"Yoohoo, Ramona, over here!"

She turned to look and saw Delilah Travis waving her arms wildly over her head from behind a refreshment table. Her husband Dewey stood next to her. Ramona did not want to go over to them, but felt she had no choice since Delilah had already spotted her. So she put on her brightest and most confident smile and walked over to them.

"Well hello, Delilah. Dewey. Great day for the meet, isn't it? This table looks great. I'm sure these snacks will be gone in no time!" Ramona chirped, trying to keep her tone light.

"Oh yes, of course they will," Delilah said, ignoring the compliment. "But more importantly, where is that husband of yours with those shirts? Why isn't he back yet?"

Ramona opened her mouth to answer, but Dewey spoke first.

"You know, Ralph passed our pad the other day on his way to *Leaps and Bounds*. Said he wasn't sure about how to get there. I told him I could get him there and back in no time flat," Dewey blustered.

"I know that part of the stream like I know the back of my hand."

"Really, Dewey?" Ramona said. "I'm sure Ralph would have been relieved to have you show him the way. Did he turn down your offer?"

"Naw," Dewey snorted. "Matter of fact, he asked me to go with him, but I said there was no way. Had yard work an' stuff to do, ya know? Delilah wants our pad to look like it came out of a magazine. Also thought I'd stick around just in case Coach Stone needed me for anything."

"Oh, I see," Ramona mumbled, looking away from him so he would not see the anger in her eyes.

"Yeah. Hope Coach knew what he was doin' when he let Ralph go for the shirts. Boys'll be pretty disappointed if they don't have 'em."

Ramona suddenly raised her eyes to meet Dewey's, no longer caring if he saw the anger in them.

"I'm sure you're as fast as you say you are, Dewey. And I'm sure the chores your wife wants you to do around the house are much more important than helping Ralph find his way to *Leaps and Bounds*. Don't underestimate my husband. He'll get those shirts to the team one way or another, with or without your help."

Dewey looked like he had been slapped in the face.

"What's more, I have total faith in Ralph, and I guess Coach Stone does too, or he wouldn't have trusted him to go in the first place. He'll be here. Bet on it," Ramona snapped. With that she turned her back to him and headed to the spectators' bleachers. She was glad that he could not hear the question that repeated itself in her head.

But would he get here in time?

———— ((◊)) ————

"Hey Marcus, here's another one," Bobby cawed as he dropped another gold shirt into the tattered cardboard box. The seven birds had searched the stream all the way back to *Leaps and Bounds*. They had found most of them floating in the water or wedged between the rocks.

"How many do we have so far?" Bobby asked.

Marcus counted the soggy shirts piled on top of each other inside the box.

"Twenty-five!" he crowed. "That's all of them. Now let's get them to Ralph."

With Max and Simon carrying the box between them in their beaks, the seven crows rose into the sky and headed toward the spot where they had left Ralph. Marcus was confused when he saw no sign of him.

"I can't believe that we found the shirts and lost Ralph," he said.

"So what do we do, Marcus?" Max asked. "How will we get them to Ralph now?"

Marcus was silent for a minute, and then said, "We keep looking. Let's go." And back into the sky they went.

For several minutes they glided low over the stream as it circled around the woods, but none of the crows spotted the small frog.

It was finally Marcus who saw him. Ralph was standing at the edge of the stream where it met the shortcut through the woods on the other side. His hand was over his eyes to shield them from the sun as he searched the sky for the crows. He didn't see them dive down behind him.

"Ralph, where were you? We've been looking for you. How did you get this far in such a short time?" Marcus asked.

Sorry for the confusion he had caused, Ralph told the crows about Ira, Jeremy and the shortcut through the woods.

"Ok, no harm done. Glad we found you. We've got all the shirts, Ralph. Now let's get you to where you need to be.

If we hurry, we can make it back before the meet starts. Hop onto my back and hold on!" Marcus said, lifting the small green frog into the sky with him as they headed toward Muddyville Middle School.

Chapter Sixteen
The Meet

"OKAY, LISTEN UP, guys," Coach Stone said. "We start in fifteen minutes. You all know what you have to do. Any questions?"

Eddy Travis shouted, "Yeah Coach, where are our shirts? We were supposed to have them by now. Where's Ribbit's dad?"

Coach was asking himself the same question, but said, "I'm sure Mr. Ribbit is going to be here any minute, Eddy. But remember one thing. Shirts or no shirts, you guys are a team, and a good one. Work hard and work together. That's what makes winners. Now go loosen up."

Reggie walked away from the group, feeling humiliated and disappointed. His father had never let him down before. Where was he? As he stretched his legs, Eddy Travis came up beside him.

"Hey Ribbit, I told you your old man wouldn't be able to get those shirts here on time. If Coach was smart he woulda known that my dad could get the job done right. Big mistake," Eddy sneered.

"The meet didn't start yet, did it, Travis?" Reggie stood up and lunged forward, his face close to Eddy's. "You say anything about my dad and I'll knock you out. Keep your mouth shut unless you know what you're talking about. He'll be here," Reggie said, sounding much more confident than he felt.

At exactly 12 noon, the loudspeakers over the athletic field crackled to life and the announcer said, "Runners participating in the 100 yard dash, please take your places on the track." The first event was about to begin, and Ralph was still nowhere in sight.

In the bleachers, Ramona's heart sank as she watched kids from each of the three middle schools get into their stances, ready to run. On the sidelines, Reggie stood with his team and Coach Stone, wanting to be anywhere but there. Not only was he embarrassed for his father, but he was worried as well. *What had happened to him?*

With all the activity going on behind Muddyville Middle School, no one noticed the seven crows that landed on the concrete sidewalk in the front of the building. And no one noticed the small green frog that sat on the back of one of them.

Ralph hopped off of Marcus's back, and took the box from Max and Simon. "I can't even begin to thank you for what you did for me today," he said to them. "I never would have made it back here in time without the help of good friends like you."

Marcus cawed and flapped his wing at him as they listened to the voice on the loudspeaker. "You don't need to thank us. That's what friends are for. Now get back there with those shirts before the starting gun goes off. I hope your son and his friends know how lucky they are to have you on their team."

As Marcus and the other crows took off into the air, Ralph hurried toward the athletic field. Hugging the cardboard box of shirts, he headed for his son and the Muddyville Middle School track team. He had made it.

Chapter Seventeen
And the Winner Is...

BY FOUR O'CLOCK on Saturday afternoon, Ralph Ribbit and his family were back at home in their den. Roxie was playing on the floor with her stuffed mouse. Ramona was sewing tiny iridescent dragonflies onto one of her daughter's sweaters. Reggie and his father were talking about the track meet.

"It's kind of disappointing that we didn't take first place. The guys from Shadybrook only beat us by 10 points," Reggie said.

"I know, son. Everyone wants to be first, but that can't always happen. If you did your best, then no one can call you a loser.

"Even though Muddyville finished in second place, I'm very proud of you. Taking first place in the pole vault and stepping up to lead the relay team to the win when Eddy Travis got hurt makes you a winner in my book," Ralph said.

"Yeah, can you believe it? He and his dad kept telling everybody that he was going to win it for Muddyville. And then he twisted his ankle fooling around and couldn't run at all."

Ralph shook his head and chuckled.

"Dad," Reggie said quietly, "those shirts really gave our team a boost. I know you went through a lot of trouble to get them back to us on time. All the kids were really impressed."

"Reggie, someday when you have your own kids, you'll understand why I did what I did, no matter how difficult it was. But you look a little sad. Still thinking about not winning the meet?" Ralph said.

"No, I feel kinda guilty about something."

"Guilty? Why?"

"Because right before the meet started, when it didn't look like you were going to show up, I was angry and embarrassed and disappointed. All I thought about was how you'd let me and the team down. I wasn't thinking about what you had to go through."

Ralph put his arm around his son's shoulders. "Don't feel guilty, Reggie. Any kid would have felt that way. I'm just glad that everything worked out in the end."

With that, Ramona put down her sewing to hand Ralph what was left of his backpack. As soon as they had returned home, he had thrown it, unopened, in its spot behind his chair.

"Ralph, why don't you clean that thing out before we throw it away," she said. "I have strainers that don't have as many holes in them as that bag does."

"Good idea, dear," Ralph chuckled as he struggled to open it.

A corner of his jacket had become caught in the zipper the last time he had closed the backpack. After a few good yanks, he got it open.

"Looks like this can go into the trash, too, Ramona," he said, holding the ruined jacket up in front of him.

"You're right, but check the pockets, just in case you left something in one of them."

Ralph didn't think there was any point in doing that. What could possibly be left that would be of any use now? But rather than argue with her, he plunged his hand into one pocket. He was surprised when it went right through a hole and down to the lining at the bottom edge of the jacket. Ralph's hand touched something, and he pulled it out to look at it.

"What's this?" he said, clutching a damp sheet of folded paper. Holding it between his thumb and index finger, Ralph gently unfolded it. The paper was wrinkled and the printing on it was smudged, but it was still readable. Ralph gasped as he showed it to Reggie and Ramona. At the top of the paper, in Coach Stone's printing, were the words *Directions to Leaps and Bounds*. And below them was a carefully drawn map of the stream.

For a few seconds, no one spoke. And then Ramona looked at Ralph, and Ralph looked at Reggie, and they all burst out laughing.

CPSIA information can be obtained
at www.ICGtesting.com
Printed in the USA
FFOW03n2024010217
31996FF